LIFE IN THE SECURITY DIRECTORATE

A SHORT STORY

ALEXANDRIA BLAELOCK

BlueMere Books
MELBOURNE, AUSTRALIA

Publisher's Note: This is a work of fiction. Names, characters, places, and incidents are a product of the author's imagination. Locations and public names are sometimes used for atmospheric purposes. Any resemblance to actual people, living or dead, or to businesses, companies, events, institutions, or locations is completely coincidental.

Copyright © 2020 Alexandria Blaelock.

All rights reserved. No part of this publication may be reproduced, distributed or transmitted in any form or by any means, including photocopying, recording, or other electronic or mechanical methods, without the prior written permission of the publisher, except in the case of brief quotations embodied in critical reviews and certain other non-commercial uses permitted by copyright law.

For permission requests, please contact enquiries@bluemerebooks.com.

Ordering Information:
Discounts are available on quantity purchases. For details, contact orders@bluemerebooks.com.

Life in the Security Directorate/Alexandria Blaelock
paperback ISBN: 978-1-925749-16-8
digital ISBN: 978-1-925749-17-5

Book Layout © BookDesignTemplates.com

LIFE IN THE SECURITY DIRECTORATE

Eve closed her eyes and leaned her forehead against the stationery cupboard door. Most of her days were pretty shitty, but for some reason, this one was shittier than most.

Maybe not the shittiest day of her life, that was probably the day she'd been born.

After she passed the Genomics Bureau postnatal testing, her parents had quickly signed her and all her rights over to the State. She was remanded to the State Academy of Cultural Regulation while her parents tried to live down the shame of producing what was colloquially known as a superhero.

She took a deep calming breath.

What was it she needed right now?

Black Earl Grey tea with a thin slice of lemon. And a lemon shortbread biscuit to go with it. In a nice vintage, rose-patterned bone china cup and saucer.

She pulled the cupboard door open, and there it was, steaming gently on top of a stack of notebooks.

She smoothed a few stray mouse-brown loose hairs back into her long ponytail and took her tea back to her desk.

Kicking off her sensible shoes, she pulled open the bottom drawer of her broken pedestal unit, pulled out a small cushion which she placed on her desk and propped her feet up on it.

Drawing the silence around her like a cloak of invisibility, she closed her eyes and inhaled the tea's citrus aroma before taking a sip.

Designated FX-84325, she'd been given all the love and care you'd expect of a State-run Academy - bullying, intensive education, hard physical work, mind control and so on.

Instead of being trained to fit in, the children were intensively trained to stand out. At least they were if they didn't die during basic training.

Survivors had no choice but to join the Protection Squadron. The terrifyingly impassive guardians of whatever the State named the public good.

No friends or family to influence their rigid, unbiased and unthinking law enforcement.

During the fiercely competitive initial training, she hadn't displayed a useful skill, like reading or influencing minds, blowing up or moving heavy loads or getting places really fast.

Subsequently, she'd been redesignated FG-84325, and shunted into general training for low-level operatives; colloquially known as goons.

She rotated her shoulders a few times and rocked her head back and forth across them to try and relieve the tension and stiffness.

As bad as her subsequent life had been, Eve was grateful she'd been declared faulty and expelled from the programme.

As a failed superhero, she at least had the chance of a somewhat normal life.

It wasn't easy though - the Directorate sent out undercover agents as failed superheroes too, so you were greeted with suspicion wherever you went. It was very rare anyone would trust or want to get to know you.

Now designated Eve, the State mandated name for failed female operatives, with a permanent record of attendance at superhero school, the population treated her as warily as a jaguar zoo escapee.

Not to mention that expulsion left her standing outside the school gates with just the clothes on her back.

No family, no money, no support. Presumably, given the training, the idea was to ensure you didn't survive on your own.

She dunked her biscuit in the tea and savoured the flavour as it slowly dissolved on her tongue.

Eve had always been lucky. She'd always been able to lay her hands on whatever she needed. Whether that was an extra food ration, a safe place to hide, or a helping hand. Or maybe that was her superpower.

Undetected, because she needed it to be.

For her, it was a pretty useful power to have, even though it wasn't always reliable. She wasn't sure how need was determined, or what would meet that need.

Or where the stuff came from. Or given it disappeared when she was done needing it, what happened to it.

She took a deep breath and stretched as she let it out in a sigh.

Her ability to quickly obtain required supplies with a minimum of fuss had earned her a tiny, yet private office in the warehouse.

It was gloomy, full of broken furniture and a long way from where the business action happened.

But it was all hers.

Plus, her unwavering cheerfulness in the face of constant doubt had gained her a certain amount of tolerance from her colleagues.

She would always be an outsider, but she was treated reasonably well and accepted at company functions.

Though, fearing alcohol-fuelled reprisals for Protection Squad activities, she always managed to leave before the drinking started in earnest.

She didn't know for sure, but it made sense the Squad would monitor her activities more carefully than normals, so she'd been vigilant.

In general, she lived a quiet life, skirting the fringes of other people's lives. She kept to herself, dressed and acted to avoid attention, and tried not to use her power unless it was necessary.

But she was lonely. She worked alone, then went home alone, to her tiny apartment full of smiling stuffed animals. She bought cookbooks from exotic places she would never be permitted to visit and cooked single-serve meals.

After dinner, she curled up in a blanket, reading borrowed books, living an adventurous kind of life with close friends forbidden to her.

Imagining she was allowed a boyfriend, someone to kiss and openly share her feelings with.

Today's borrowed tea and biscuit was relatively minor - a quiet moment outside of normal. Once she'd been followed into a building, and exited from another in someone else's body.

She sighed again, put the empty teacup down, and massaged her temples. Just for a moment, she imagined another life.

One where the State didn't monitor and control the people. Where there was no such thing as a Protection Squad, and people lived their lives freely and openly.

What would that be like?

Standing up, she stretched again and walked across the room to the window overlooking the warehouse. The sun was shining, birds were singing, and a warm, soft floral breeze blew through a crack in the glass.

Given the opportunity, she'd have climbed out the window to see what that other life was like, but the bars made that impossible.

For the moment she'd satisfy herself with a borrowed breath of fresh air.

The stiff office door scraped and jittered as someone tried to open it.

Eve turned away from the window and walked towards her desk. By the time she got there, the room had reverted to its usual dingy appearance.

The sunny exterior view faded to a dirty safety glass window overlooking the warehouse. The cushion, teacup and saucer also disappeared.

An odour of must rolled over the light scent of flowers.

She stepped back into her shoes, smoothed her grey pencil skirt down and kicked the pedestal drawer shut.

Then picked up a notebook covered in a girly cartoon pattern from her neat and clean desk, along with a pencil topped by a half-used rabbit eraser.

She pasted a cheerful smile on her face and was ready to take on whoever came through the door.

It suddenly gave way, and a tall, well-dressed muscular man fell through, tripping a few steps forward to collide with her.

She deftly caught and held him to stop him falling over. Trying not to inhale his brisk outdoorsy scent, she let him catch his balance.

He quickly took a step back. While it was probably for his own protection, Eve was grateful to have more air around her.

"I'm sorry, the door's sticky. I've called the maintenance department, but it's a very low priority."

He smiled and waved a hand in its direction, "there's no need. It's not your fault."

Eve smiled a small smile and bowed her head in acknowledgement.

"I'm Adam, I'm here about the Statutory Department's order for half a pallet of copy paper."

Eve looked a little more closely at him. His name labelled him a failed superhero just like her, but his clothing suggested he was an agent.

She'd never met another failure and didn't know what to expect.

She schooled her face, trying not to look too alarmed or interested. She was fairly sure she hadn't done anything to raise suspicion, but he could still be there for a random audit.

She put her notebook and pencil down and nodded professionally. "I've prepared your order for dispatch. If you'll follow me, I'll show you where it is."

She opened the warehouse door and led him down the steel stairs, his eyes boring holes in her back.

Not literally, of course, he was a failure too, but her recently relaxed shoulders started tensing up again anyway.

As they walked through the racked stock, Eve was at war with herself.

On one side, she was eaten up with curiosity about who he was and how he came to be there.

Even though she was essentially quarantined from the normals, she thought someone might have mentioned there was another failure in the building.

Or were there so many of them by now that it barely rated a mention?

On the other side, who was he, and why was he there? Was he auditing her?

Was he involved in some other State ordered action, even if he was only the copy boy? Did he know she was an Eve?

How did he fail out of the Academy?

But as they moved further away from her office, the silence lengthened. All too soon they'd reached the stacked trolley, and it was too late to ask anything at all.

Eve put her cheerful face back on and nodded her ponytailed head at the trolley, "here we are - all stacked up and ready to go. Can you manage from here?"

He gave the trolley an experimental push and smiled ruefully. "I think I'll be okay with the trolley, but I'm new here and have no idea how to get back to my workstation."

Eve nodded once, "are you on the Statutory Department floor?"

"I guess so."

"Fine, I can take you back," she gestured toward the side of the warehouse, "this way."

He took the trolley, made a small u-turn to get it going, and headed in the direction she'd pointed.

Determined not to lose this second opportunity, she stepped up and walked beside him, "have you been with us long?"

"About a week. I'm here collating some documents to send to the Office of Public Enlightenment."

"I see, do you work for Public Enlightenment?"

Adam snorted, "do you really think with the name Adam I'd be working for Public Enlightenment? I'm just an admin temp; here to fetch coffee, sharpen pencils and do the copying."

Eve pursed her lips for a moment. He seemed very open about his failure, but other than that, it was too soon to trust him, "I understand."

"I heard there's an Eve here somewhere, do you know where I might find her?"

Eve gasped and stepped back, what did he want with an Eve?

And did he want an Eve, or did he want her?

Adam turned to look quizzically at her suddenly shuttered face.

"I am Eve, what do you want with me."

He held out in supplication, "I'm sorry, I didn't mean to scare you. I just overheard a conversation about you and wanted to meet you. I've never met another failure before."

His answer was a little too much like what she wanted to hear.

If she was an agent, it'd be the kind of thing she'd say to try and gain trust. But at the same time, it was exactly what she'd been thinking about him.

Was this her superpower trying to give her what she needed?

She frowned at him, "then you'll know that just makes you seem more like an agent than a failure. What did you overhear?"

"Essentially, that you seem so nice and normal, they can't believe you're a superhero. They were speculating that something went wrong during your postnatal testing and you'd been misdiagnosed. I've never heard anything like it before."

Eve slumped back against the racking. If, in fact, any of that was true, it was high praise from her colleagues. But could he or they really be trusted?

Her empty heart really hoped so.

She needed a chocolate, and wondering vaguely what he might need, reached hopefully into the stock behind her. She pulled out a packet and without looking at it, opened it and offered him first go.

"Oh my god, it's salted macadamias, my favourite! Where did you get them?"

That answered the question about whether she could pick up what other people needed. "I spend most of my time down here, and it's too tiresome to keep running up the stairs to the office, so I stash snacks about the place. Would you like something to drink?"

Adam smiled, "how about a delicious can of State Regulated Cola then?"

To give her story some substance, she handed over the nuts, darted out of sight round around the rack and came back with two lukewarm cans.

He laughed, clenched the nut packet between his teeth and reached for a can.

He opened it and handed it back before taking the other. "I guess your colleagues are right, you *are* too normal to be a superhero."

Eve blushed prettily and put on her cheerful face, "you're too kind. What about you, were you misdiagnosed as well?"

Going by the shock in his face, it was probably a little too intimate too soon. She took a quick gulp of the drink and came up choking.

He pounded her back to help clear her airways.

Once her coughs had subsided, she said "I'm sorry Adam, that was very presumptuous of me. Please forget I asked."

"No, it's not that," he said, sipping his drink, "it's just that like you, I'm not used to people talking to me."

He hooked a big box from the bottom rack with his foot and gestured for her to sit before snagging one for himself.

"Partway through the skills assessment, I became ill and lost my ability. The Academy tried a variety of treatments, but couldn't bring it back."

He shrugged, "after a couple of years of experimentation, I was invalided out."

It was a plausible story, but it had taken her decades of hard work to make the pitiful career progress she'd made.

How did he come to be wearing a high-quality suit working with classified information for the Office of Public Enlightenment?

She took a more careful drink. "So you work for the Security Directorate now?"

He looked at her in disbelief, "I'm sorry, I don't get how you came to that conclusion?"

Eve gestured at his suit pants, "well, you're an overly confident, fit and healthy failed superhero wearing a decent suit. Why would anyone think you were anything other than an agent?"

He snorted, "I can see why you'd think that, but I'm Adam Rochester of the Signals Department Rochesters. They didn't renounce me when I was invalided out of the Academy. Came close though."

Well, that made all the difference - rich boy from a cultural elite family with all the benefits that brought him.

"So you just get preferential treatment because your family's high up in the political hierarchy?"

"Well not entirely, the law is still the law, regardless of who your family is. I'm still Adam - I can't be a superhero, and I can't live a normal life."

He closed his eyes for a moment and took a swig from the can. "My family tolerates me, but I'm still a failure in their eyes. It just means they're compelled to take care of me, though they've made it plain they expect me to take care of myself and not drain their resources."

He smiled evilly, "I bet they regret setting up a trust fund for me as well as not renouncing me."

Eve drained her drink and left the empty can on the rack. Dare she conduct an experiment of her own?

Failed superheroes aren't permitted physical contact, but she needed to know whether he was friend or foe, so she daringly nudged his shoulder with her own.

"I sometimes wonder what it would be like to live somewhere else where these rules don't apply don't you?"

He frowned a little, but made no mention of the contact, "I can't imagine living anywhere else, but maybe more like a normal. To have friends and parties - to be welcomed, not shunned."

They sat in companionable silence, each trying to imagine a future that wasn't State controlled.

He sighed, "I've been gone a while, I suppose I should get back to my copying."

Eve echoed his sigh, she didn't think it had been that long of a break, and agent or not, she really didn't want to let him go, "it's been nice, thanks for taking the time to chat."

She stood and placed his empty nut bag and can with her own "the goods lift is this way."

He stood, dusted his hands on his pants and kicked the boxes back into their places in the rack, "do you want me to take the rubbish?"

"No thanks, I'll get rid of it when I get back."

He gave the trolley a solid push to get it moving again, and they crossed the final space to the lift.

Eve pushed the up button, "if the lift opened to a parallel universe, would you get in?"

He glanced at her, "Now who sounds like an agent?"

She laughed, "I know, but what's the worst that can happen? We get euthanised?"

"Don't you think they'd torture you for information or something before they kill you?"

"I don't know, it's not something you hear about, is it? Not knowing, and imagining is worse than knowing for sure."

The lift binged, "last chance" she shouted, "in or out?"

He opened his mouth, she wasn't sure whether it was to scream or answer her question, but the lift doors opened to reveal the padded walls of the goods lift, and it was too late.

She waited for him to manoeuvre the trolley into the carriage before entering herself and pushing the button for the 57th floor. She stood to the side, facing Adam, hands clasped in front of her.

He flinched as it shuddered and dropped slightly before starting its ascent. "Why would you even think about parallel universes?" he asked.

"I think it's the nature of all humans, superhero or normal, to seek freedom and happiness. What about you and your friends and parties? Aren't you tired of living alone?"

"I suppose. But, given I'm a Rochester, I'm never really alone. Though I get all the Rochester obligations without the benefits. It would be nice to please myself occasionally."

"Can I take that as Yes! I'll get off at the closest parallel universe?"

He jiggled the trolley as he thought, "You know what, I might be wrong, but I can't see how it could be worse than here. Aside from arriving there with nothing."

"Like the ultimate refugee - nothing to lose and everything to gain."

He laughed awkwardly, "yes, I suppose so."

The lift binged as they approached their destination, and Adam bunched his muscles, preparing to push the trolley out into the corridor.

The doors opened to reveal a lush green meadow, drenched in sunshine. Eve pushed the button that held the doors open.

The wind bent the grass, pushing the fresh scent of the open countryside into the carriage. A butterfly flew in, found no flowers and flew out again.

Adam's jaw dropped, and he rubbed his eyes as if he couldn't believe what he was seeing.

She smiled at him, "we've reached our destination. Do you want to please yourself enough to follow me?"

His once-friendly face contorted, and he snarled, "I knew you were too good to be true."

It seemed he was an undercover agent after all. He tried to get out from behind the trolley, but right now, she needed him to stay where he was, and the trolley wheels obliged.

He lunged at her as she stepped out onto the grass, but he just succeeded in dislodging boxes of paper and fencing himself in.

Perhaps he was just afraid, "this really is your last chance Adam, once the doors close, they'll reopen, and you'll be back at the Statutory Department. Neither one thing nor the other."

"I don't know what you've done to me, but there is no other universe. I'm placing you under arrest - get back in this lift."

The wind pulled her hair loose from her ponytail, and it crackled around her head like electricity.

"You know I can't do that Adam. My sad life was over the minute you entered my building. I don't know where I am, or if my power will work here. But no matter what, I'm better off here."

He snarled and lunged again.

"This really is your last chance Adam. We don't even have to stay together. You can make your own path to your future."

"There is nothing for me there that I don't have here. For all I know, it will be worse there. You'll probably be eaten by lions."

She smiled sadly, "thanks for showing me what I missed Adam. I wish you a future of freedom and happiness."

Eve didn't need an escape route, so she raised a hand in farewell, let the lift doors close with a final clunk and disappear.

She stretched and took a deep breath of fresh air. It didn't matter where she went, so she closed her eyes and spun around a few times, then started walking. She couldn't wait to see what this world had to offer.

THE END

ABOUT THE AUTHOR

Alexandria Blaelock writes stories, some of them for *Ellery Queen's Mystery Magazine* and *Pulphouse Fiction Magazine*. She's also written four self-help books applying business techniques to personal matters like getting dressed, cleaning house, and feeding your friends.

As a recovering Project Manager, she's probably too fond of sticking to plan. She lives in a forest because she enjoys birdsong, the scent of gum leaves and the sun on her face. When not telecommuting to parallel universes from her Melbourne based imagination, she watches K-dramas, talks to animals, and drinks Campari. At the same time.

Discover more at www.alexandriablaelock.com.

OTHER SHORT STORIES BY ALEXANDRIA BLAELOCK

Kiss of Death
Long Weekend in the Snow
Shining Star
Phoenix Child
Ship in a Bottle
Lady of the Looking Glass
Simone Says Hands in the Air
Life in the Security Directorate
Fate in Your Hands
Love in the Security Directorate
Alma's Grace
Payton's Run
The Guardian's Vigil
The Life and Death of Carmelita Basingstoke
Balancing the Book

BOOKS BY ALEXANDRIA BLAELOCK

Stress Free Dinner Parties
Build Your Signature Wardrobe
Holistic Personal Finance
Ms Blaelock's Book of Minimally Viable Housekeeping